TUCKET'S RIDE

— ◉ —

Gary Paulsen

A YEARLING BOOK

Published by
Dell Yearling
an imprint of
Random House Children's Books
a division of
Random House, Inc.
1540 Broadway
New York, New York 10036

Visit us on the Web! www.randomhouse.com/kids

Educators and librarians, for a variety of teaching tools, visit us at www.randomhouse.com/teachers

ISBN: 0-440-41147-5

Reprinted by arrangement with Delacorte Press

Printed in the United States of America

April 1998

20 19 18 17 16 15 14 13 12

OPM

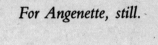

For Angenette, still.

Chapter One

Francis Tucket lay on the ridge and watched the adobe hut a hundred yards away and slightly below him. He had his rifle resting on a hump of dirt, the sights unmoving, pointed at the doorway to the hut.

"Are we going to stay here forever? I mean it's really cold. I've been cold before but not like this." A small girl and boy stood ten yards to his rear with the horse and mule, all hidden below the level of the ridge. "It just seems that since you haven't seen anything, we could go down there and get warm. There might be a stove . . ."

"Please be quiet, Lottie." Francis turned and held his hand out. "Now. We're going to wait. I heard something somewhere down there that sounded like a scream. We're going to wait and watch. Be quiet."

There was a horse in front of the hut, tied to a half-broken hitch rail. Some chickens walked around the sides pecking at the dirt. There was no dog. Three goats were tied to stakes in back of the house. The horse had a familiar saddle on its back—military cut with the bedroll in front. The horse didn't look wet, so it hadn't worked hard getting here. Then, too, Lottie was right—it was cold, so the horse wouldn't show much sweat.

All this went into Francis's eyes and registered in his thoughts automatically—along with the direction of the wind, the fact that a coyote was off to the side a couple of hundred yards away eyeing the chickens, and a hawk was circling over the yard doing the same thing. All of it in and filed away.

There. A scream—short but high. Not a man. Maybe a child or a woman.

Well. That was all Francis thought: *Well.* If it was somebody needing help, he was in a bad place to give it. One fifteen-year-old boy, a young girl and a boy with him, a horse and a mule and one rifle.

Still. He couldn't stay and not help.

It was what he got for not going west, he thought—for not taking the two children and just heading out along the Oregon Trail to find his parents and the wagon train he had been kidnapped from more than a year ago. He and the children had made a good start west, then had gotten sidetracked as they crossed the prairie, and before he knew it an early fall had caught them short of the mountains. Snow had filled all the passes.

Somebody at a trading post on the trail had said that there was a southern route down in Mexico that stayed open all year, so Francis had started south. They couldn't hope to winter in the northern prairies. He hadn't realized that taking on Lottie and her little brother, Billy, would slow him down so. He had found them, alone on the prairie, after their father had died of cholera.

It had grown warmer as they had moved south along the mountains. Still cold at night, but they had picked up some wool blankets at the trading post, and Lottie had sewn pullover coats for all of them as they moved down into the territory belonging to Mexico.

There. He heard a thump, then a scream.

"You two stay here," he called softly to Lottie. "And I mean *stay* here. I'll be back."

He slid to the left where there was a thin brush line and followed it down to the hut. The building did not have a window, which was good, because the brush line was sparse scrub oak and the goats had long before stripped away the leaves.

Now Francis was barely concealed, and ran quickly, trying to keep his moccasins quiet.

He held himself still at the side of the hut, listening. Again, a muffled sound. He checked the cap on his rifle, cocked it, and moved to the side of the door.

He was five feet from the door when he noted that the saddle on the horse had a large US stamped on the sides, and the horse had the same brand on its shoulder. It was a United States Cavalry mount. Half a question formed in his mind—what was a United States Cavalry mount doing in Mexican territory?—when the door blew open and a young woman ran out, a large man behind her. He grabbed her shoulders.

"Get back in here!"

Half a second: Her eyes were wide with terror; she had a scuff on her face where she'd been hit. The man's blue uniform shirt was ripped. He had a bloody scratch on his cheek. He was wearing a military belt with a flap-covered holster, and he saw Francis, threw the woman aside, and clawed at the holster.

"Wait . . . ," Francis got out, then saw the flap of the holster come up, the hand catch the butt of the revolver, the barrel swing toward him as the man cocked it, an explosion of smoke and noise.

Francis felt the ball cut his cheek and burn past and he shot from the hip. His rifle recoiled in his hands and he saw the ball strike the man high in the chest. He saw everything: a little puff of dust from the blue shirt as the ball hit; no blood, but dust, and then the man went backward and down to a sitting position. He looked up at Francis and said, "You've killed me," and settled on his back slowly and died.

All in three seconds. Francis stood in silent horror. He felt the sun on his back, the terrified woman standing in front of him, the goats bleating nearby, the smoke from the shots drifting off to the side. He stood there and knew that nothing would ever be the same again.

He had killed a man.

Chapter Two

"Oh, Francis, what have you done? I knew I shouldn't have let you come down here alone. Seems like if I take my eyes off you for a minute you get into all sorts of trouble. It reminds me of a cousin I had. He was always . . ." Lottie had come down the hill and started talking before she'd seen what had happened. She stopped when she saw the body.

Francis stood, still in shock.

"*¿Habla español?*" the woman said.

Francis looked at her. "What?"

"She's speaking in a different tongue," Lottie said. "Could be French. I heard a man talk French once back home. He could rattle it off so fast it made your brain blur . . ."

"Is Spanish," the woman said. "Do you speak?"

Francis shook his head. "No. Just English." He was still staring down at the dead man. "What happened here? I mean why . . ."

"He is soldier from the north." She spat the words. "He came wanting me. Dirty pig. I say no, Garza fight. He hurt Garza. Help me with him."

She moved into the hut and Francis followed. Inside there was only the light from the door. There was an earthen floor packed hard and swept, whitewashed walls, a small fireplace in the corner, a table, two chairs and a bed. A young man lay on the floor unconscious.

"Help me," she said. "He is hurt . . ."

The woman and Lottie took the man's legs and Francis took him by the shoulders. They put him on the cot. He was breathing but had blood on his head. A piece of firewood lay on the floor with blood on one end.

"Husband," she said. "Man hit him with *piñon*." She went to a shelf in one corner where an earthen jug held water. She poured some into a clay bowl, dipped a rag in it, and began wiping away the blood and dirt.

"I don't understand," Francis said in bewilderment. "What is an American soldier doing here?"

She stopped wiping and squinted at him in the dim light coming through the door. "It is the war, no?"

"War? What war?"

"There was war between Mexico and the United States."

"A war? But how can that be? I mean—"

"You did not know?"

Francis shook his head. "Never heard a word about it."

"You know," Lottie started, "come to think of it I believe I did overhear some men talking about trouble with Mexico at the trading post. Of course they weren't talking to me. Nobody talks to me. But I think one of them said to the other that he'd heard there was a problem with the borders or something. I couldn't hear well because *someone* was telling me to hurry up and leave. But I think they were—"

"And you didn't tell me?" Francis turned to her. "We're riding down into Mexico and you didn't say a word?"

"It slipped my mind. What with having to hurry and all the time having to keep quiet about things it just slipped my mind."

"Where's Billy?"

"I left him with the horse and mule."

"Maybe you'd better go check on him."

"You're just trying to get rid of me."

"No I'm not. Now go check on him while I try to figure out what to do."

"Do? Why, you've got that huge body out there to deal with, *that's* what you've got to do. I don't see any muddle on that score. Have to dig a big hole and bury him."

"Lottie . . ."

"I'm going."

Francis turned back to the woman. Her husband was breathing more regularly and starting to move his arms.

"When did the war start?" Francis asked.

She shrugged. "One day Mexican soldiers come by going to Taos. The next day *norteamericano* soldiers come by and say there is war. I hear of big battle between Santa Fe and Taos. Mexican soldiers leave, *americano* soldiers stay. Then this pig"—she pointed out the door at the body—"he came back for me. Then you come and shoot him. And now it is now."

And now, Francis thought, I have killed an American soldier. He was a bad man, true, and he shot first, but even so, I have killed him.

"You are bleeding." The woman came to him and used a clean corner of the damp cloth to wipe his cheek where the bullet had creased him.

"It's nothing. Nothing at all." Francis pushed her hand away and tried to think.

What to do?

Bury the soldier and *run*. It came into his mind as if it had always been there. Hide your tracks and cut and run. Get out before somebody finds out what happened. No one knew his name.

No. He couldn't run from *this*. Not *this*. He had to settle it first or it would be hanging over his head for the rest of his life. He leaned against the wall and moments of all that had happened to him since he had lost his family came back to him in flashes. Kidnapped by the Pawnees. Escaping them with the help of the mountain man, Mr. Grimes. Jason Grimes had rescued Francis and had taught him most of what he needed to survive, yet they had parted. Parted ways because of a killing.

"Where is the army?" Francis asked the woman, who had gone back to work on her husband. "How far are they?"

"They are in Taos. Where the pig came from."

"How far is this Taos place?"

"One day of walking not so fast."

He thought about distances. You could walk thirty miles a day without working too hard. Walking not so fast might mean a lot less. Fifteen or twenty miles. An easy day on horses.

There it was then. He'd have to take the body and find the army and explain what had happened.

Stupid, he thought. No, much more than that. The man had come here alone to do a stupid, terrible thing, then had made it worse by shooting at Francis without thinking and Francis had made it worse by getting involved in the first place. I should have kept riding, he thought, not come when I'd heard the scream.

But he couldn't have done that either.

He beckoned to the woman to follow him outside. "Would you help me? I have to roll his body in his blanket and tie it over his horse."

"Drag it out to the desert and leave for coyotes."

Francis shook his head. "No. I'll need to bring the body back to Taos."

He started to untie the blanket from the soldier's bedroll on his saddle.

Crazy, all of it. Just plain insane.

─ Chapter Three ─

As it turned out, they didn't have to go all the way to Taos alone with the body.

Loading it had been hard, but finally, with the woman and Lottie helping while Billy held the trooper's horse, they had boosted the dead man belly down over the saddle and tied him in with rope. The horse didn't like it much, didn't like the smell of death, and Francis had to keep him on a short lead as they left the adobe hut and headed south.

The country was dry but pretty. There were high bluffs on the left, and they had not gone more than five miles when they came on a small settlement along a flowing river. There were no people evident, though there were tilled fields and some goats and pigs in pens. Francis stopped to water the horses. They could not set too fast a pace with the dead soldier's body bouncing across his horse. Several times Francis had a struggle to keep the trooper's horse from running away.

"It's spooky here," Lottie said, and even Billy, who sometimes went two or three days without saying a word, said, "Ha'nts."

Lottie took a deep breath and began, "I remember one time when Ma and Pa were both alive and we were back east somewhere, we were pulling the wagon and saw all kinds of shooting stars, and Pa thought they were spooky but Ma didn't and they had an argument about it that lasted nigh on three days . . ."

Carrying a body didn't help, Francis thought—it made everything spooky. He gigged the horses to get them going again; they thought they were going to spend the night in the settlement and were reluctant to leave. He had to kick with his heels and jerk on the horse carrying the body until he finally got them going. The mule came along peacefully, for which Francis was grateful.

Three miles out of the settlement, still a solid ten miles from Taos, they ran into the patrol of soldiers.

There were seven troopers and an officer leading. They came in from the west out of the desert, not on the north–south trail. Their mounts looked done in. Even at a distance Francis could see the horses wobbling, walking too loosely.

I could still run, Francis thought, watching them come toward the trail. We have good stock, fresh horses, and the mule would outdistance any horse alive. I could still run.

But he knew he wouldn't.

The troopers cut the trail half a mile and more ahead of them. They started to turn and head toward Taos. Then one of them saw Francis and called to the others, and they all turned and waited, not wanting to push their horses any more than they had to.

When Francis was still fifty yards away one of the men said, "Hey. He's pulling Flannagan's mount. I know the blaze and one white stocking. And there's a body on it!"

The patrol kicked their exhausted mounts into motion and approached Francis and the children with weapons ready. With a start, Francis remembered that he had never reloaded his rifle. He had been so distraught that he had forgotten all about it. Not that it would help him much with eight soldiers, all weapons ready. He'd be dead before he hit the ground.

"What is all this?" the officer asked, pulling up across the trail in front of Francis to block his way. As Francis stopped, the officer rode closer and looked under the blanket. "It's Flannagan all right. How did this happen?"

For once Lottie was quiet. Francis thought quickly. If he told the truth, would they just shoot him? Or should he lie now and tell the truth later, or would that make them even angrier?

He decided to tell the truth.

"I shot him."

"*You* shot him?"

"Yes, sir. He was trying to force a Mexican woman and I surprised him. He drew his cap and ball and shot at me and I just pulled the trigger. I didn't want to shoot him. It just happened."

"It just happened . . ."

"Yes, sir. In self-defense."

"Self-defense . . ." The officer looked at the body on the horse again, then back at Francis. "Who *are* you?"

"My name is Francis Tucket. Over a year ago I was with my family heading west on the Oregon Trail and I was kidnapped by Pawnees. I escaped and tried to head after them, and on the way I found these two young ones . . ."

The officer shook his head. "Just the name for now. And one more thing. We're still fighting the Mexicans. What are you doing here, in the middle of it?"

"I didn't know there was a war . . ." Francis told him how they had hit the closed passes of the north and drifted south looking for a way through to the West.

"Some drift. You must have come five hundred miles."

"Closer to six, I think. I've been keeping track by day."

"Well, Francis Tucket, I'm going to have to take that rifle and put you under confinement until we can get to the bottom of this."

Francis shook his head. "I'll take the confinement, but I can't give you my rifle."

It was a tight moment. The rifle had been with him constantly, except for when the Indians had captured him and again when two men had surprised him sleeping. It was like an extension of his arm, his mind, and he had no intention of releasing it again, voluntarily or otherwise.

The officer moved to the side to give his troopers a clearer field of fire if they needed it. "I can't have a man under arrest with a loaded rifle . . ."

Francis nodded. "It's not loaded. I didn't reload it after I killed . . . after I fired it last."

The officer thought, looking at Francis and the children, then nodded. "All right." He turned in his saddle. "Sergeant O'Rourke!"

"Sir!"

"Form an escort around the prisoners."

"Sir!"

"Trooper Delaney!"

"Yes, Sergeant!"

"You will take the mount with Flannagan's body in tow!"

"Yes, Sergeant!"

The troopers moved their tired mounts to a line on each side of Francis and Lottie and Billy, who were still on the mule. The trooper named Delaney took the horse with the body from Francis and they all moved out. The officer started in the lead but soon dropped back alongside Francis.

"You say Flannagan was forcing a Mexican woman?"

Before Francis could answer, Lottie cut loose. She'd been silent all this while—an unnatural state for her—and she blasted the officer.

"He was being 'rageous, that soldier, simply 'rageous. Back home in Esther County they would have just taken him out and let the pigs eat him. Francis here saved that woman something awful and it ain't right you come along with all your guns and 'rest him like he was bad. He isn't bad. He's good. And that man shot at him, look at his face, see? He saved us from a fate worse than death and he saved that woman the same way. Seems like you ought to give him a medal for shooting—"

"Lottie, hold it, all right?" Francis turned and held his finger to his lips. She stopped.

"She's something when she gets going, isn't she?" The officer smiled. "Reminds me of my sister. Always knows what's right and not afraid to tell you."

Francis nodded. "She's right most of the time. Just sometimes she takes a while to get it all out."

They rode in silence for a bit. Francis's horse fretted at walking slowly with the tired cavalry mounts, and the mule picked up on it and tried to get ahead. Francis had to fight him back.

"Mules," the officer said. "Good until you need them and then they get stubborn."

"This one is all right. They just don't want to go slow. Your horses are shot."

The officer nodded. "We've been almost a hundred and fifty miles on this patrol. Looking for the Mexican Army. I told my commandant they had gone south but he still wanted to check to the north."

Francis nodded. "I haven't seen any sign of an army." He looked at the officer. "What's your name?"

"Brannigan."

Francis shook his head. "Brannigan, Flannagan, O'Rourke—why all the Irish names?"

"We're an Irish militia out of Missouri, called up for the war. We're coming through here on our way south."

"Why were we at war with Mexico?"

Brannigan snorted. "The truth is, we just want their land. They own the whole West, including California and up into the prairies, all of Texas. Those rubberneck politicians back east wanted it so they trumped up this war. It wasn't much of a war. But there are still skirmishes going on."

More silence. Francis broke it this time. "What will happen to us?"

Brannigan shook his head. "I'm not sure. Flannagan is not from my troop. He's over at K Troop so I don't know much about him except that I've heard he's a bad one to . . ." He looked around at Lottie and Billy. "A bad one to do what you caught him at. He probably deserved shooting ten times over. So I expect there won't be a problem. Still, it's not my decision. The commanding officer will have to decide."

"Oh. Well, I'm sorry I had to do it but the way it happened . . ." Francis trailed off. In the distance he could see what looked like a large earth-colored building, or many buildings tied together, some on top of others. Like adobe huts stacked up.

"What's that?"

Brannigan squinted. "That's the Taos pueblo. Just on the other side is Taos. That's where we're going."

"Who lives there?"

"The Taos Indians."

"Indians?" Francis thought of the Pawnees, and then how he could load his rifle.

Brannigan saw the concern and chuckled.

"They're not like the Plains Indians. These are more settled. They farm instead of roam and hunt."

"More civilized?"

Another laugh. "In many ways they are far more civilized than we are . . ."

Chapter Four

"Take him out and hang him."

Francis stood, not believing, almost not hearing.

They were in the commandant's office in a building on the side of the central plaza. Except that to Francis it seemed more like a saloon. The room, the building, and the man sitting in front of him were entirely devoted to drinking. Bottles lined every shelf on every wall. There was a barrel of whiskey in one corner and a rack filled with bottles of wine in another.

Francis had seen men drunk before, and he'd

seen men swill whiskey like water at the trading posts, but he had never seen anybody as drunk as the commandant. Or maybe he should say as drunk and still alive. The man wasn't sitting at his desk so much as weaving at it and his speech was slurred.

"I think, sir, that under the circumstances, we should waive . . ." Lieutenant Brannigan was standing next to Francis, and he spoke in a slow, measured tone. Lottie and Billy stood back by the door.

"Right now. Take him out in the plaza and hang him from one of those big cottonwoods out there."

"But, sir . . ."

"No buts. What are the rules if a Mexican partisan kills a trooper?"

"Sir . . ."

"The rules?"

"Summary execution, sir."

"And did this boy or did not this boy shoot and kill Trooper Flannagan?"

"Yes, sir, but . . ."

"By his own admission?"

"Yes, sir, but there were extenuating circumstances . . ."

"Doesn't matter. Take him out and hang him."

"What about the children?"

"Hang them as well." The commandant took a long swallow of something in a tin cup that looked and smelled like tequila. "Hang everybody in the plaza for all I care. It would clear the plaza of riff-raff . . ."

He leaned back and closed his eyes and for a second Francis thought he was thinking. But his breathing grew regular, and after a few moments Francis realized he had passed out cold.

"Well," Brannigan said in a low voice. "I thought that went well, didn't you?"

"Went well?" Lottie had been silent throughout, mostly because she was in shock. She took a deep breath. "He's going to have us hanged. I wouldn't call that going very well for us. I'm never going to see eleven years old and you think that's a good way for things to go? I haven't even learned how to . . . how to do anything, and they're going to string us up. You call that going well? I don't think so. Going well would be if Francis took us out of here. I just wish he hadn't had to shoot that stupid soldier . . ."

"You're not going to hang." Lieutenant Brannigan held his hand over her mouth. "He won't remember a thing he said tomorrow." He turned to

Francis. "Just keep her quiet now and let me handle this."

He turned to the door and called, "Corporal Antrim, come in here, please."

A redheaded trooper whose face was covered with freckles came into the office. "Yes, sir?"

"Commandant Donovan is napping, as you can see."

"Yes, sir."

"He was very tired."

"Yes, sir. He often is."

Brannigan nodded. "Yes. He works very hard. But just before he went to sleep he disposed of the difficulty of the shooting of Trooper Flannagan. Since the situation was to all events and purposes a tragic accident, Commandant Donovan has decided to let the matter drop."

"Yes, sir."

"Flannagan will be buried with full military honors."

"Yes, sir."

"Write up a report that states what the commandant has done for his signature when he comes to . . . awakens, will you?"

"Yes, sir."

"That will be all, Corporal."

The clerk left, and Brannigan looked at the commandant with open disgust, shook his head, and turned to Francis. "You mustn't think all officers are bad because of him. Some are very good at what they do. Well, he won't remember any of this. He'll think he made all the decisions himself when Corporal Antrim gives him the report to sign."

Brannigan opened the door again and led them outside. It was late afternoon, coming in to evening, and the light filtered through the cottonwoods on the plaza in the center of town. The leaves were gone because it was fall, but the hazy light seen through the limbs had an eerie quality.

Francis shivered. For a few moments he'd actually thought he was going to be hanged. He could feel the rope tightening around his neck. He couldn't shake the feeling. "What happens to us now?"

Brannigan stood by the horses with one hand on the mule's forehead, rubbing it idly. "You are free to go, and I do mean go. Flannagan was by all reports a complete scalawag, but he may have a friend or two who will think poorly of you for killing him. And it's best if the commandant never sees you again. No sense reminding him of what has happened."

"I understand."

"I will arrange for some grain for your stock and provisions for you. Then you just keep on going. Head south and west. In about thirty miles you'll come to a river, and you can follow it to Santa Fe. You will find the western trail you were looking for out of Santa Fe."

"Is there danger from the Mexicans?"

Brannigan shook his head. "Not for you and the children. The war has moved to the south and we've been left behind to administer. Generally people have just gone back to living their lives—most of them didn't want the war in the first place and are glad to have it moving on. Stick to the traveled roads and you'll be fine."

He turned and pointed. "Take your horse and mule to the livery and freight area south of town and they'll give you some grain and food. Tell them Lieutenant Brannigan said to provision you."

"Thank you—for everything." They shook hands. Then Francis put the children on the mule.

"No trouble," Brannigan said, as Francis mounted. "Flannagan brought it on himself. It's too bad you have to leave in a hurry. I think you would benefit from a visit to the Taos pueblo. They are a remarkable people. They have learned how to live and flourish in a place most people couldn't even pass through. You could learn much from them . . . Well," he said, "good luck to you." He saluted as they rode away. "Have all the luck there is . . ."

Chapter Five

Francis wouldn't consider going out to the pueblo to visit the Indians. He knew that not all Indians were bad, that in fact most of them were just decent people, but he had been captured by some, and held prisoner by some, and had fought some others in his mind, and he found that he was just more peaceful if he went his way and let them go theirs.

He couldn't shake the feeling of the noose around his neck, and he kept thinking about it. Wondering. What if the commandant hadn't been that drunk, and hadn't passed out, and remembered when he had come to, and decided to find them and hang them anyway? Francis paused before they left the plaza to reload his rifle, setting the butt on his left stirrup while he pushed the ball home with the ramrod. When they were moving again the thought of being hanged came back. Fretful thinking. He kept shaking his head to clear the thoughts out.

"What's the matter with you?" Lottie and Billy had been on the mule's back so long that they had almost evolved into a part of the mule. Lottie would often sit sideways on the packsaddle to "keep my autheritis from acting up." Sometimes she lay across the mule, sometimes sat forward on his neck. Once Francis had looked back to find both Billy and Lottie standing up on the mule's back, smiling at him. It just kept plodding, following Francis's horse. "You look like you up and died. . . ."

"I keep thinking on being hanged."

Lottie shrugged. "That's all done now, way I see it. Ma used to say when a thing's done it's done and it doesn't do any good to fret on it and the hanging business is all done. Besides, we're gone from it now anyway and where are we going to sleep tonight?"

Lottie had a way of running things together that made them seem somehow logical. To be done with getting hanged and worrying about where to sleep seemed perfectly natural.

"Want to eat." Billy spoke, and Francis smiled. That was two days in a row. Billy was getting positively talkative.

"We'll get some grain for the horses and then find a spot with some wood and water and make camp."

"I don't think so." Lottie looked at the country around them. "I believe the last time this country had water was when the great flood happened and you know when you think about that it makes you wonder on who's telling stories. I mean, how big would an ark have to be to get *everything* in it? And not just one, but two. Two buffalo, two mountain lions, two coyotes, two gophers, two ants, two mosquitoes, two horseflies, two ticks—and why did he include mosquitoes and ticks, I ask you? Seems Noah must have been stupid wanting to keep flies and ticks and mosquitoes around. Don't you think he was crazy? I mean, if it was me and I had a chance to get rid of horseflies, I'd drop them in a second. Right over the side. Did you ever watch them bite? They take a real chunk out of your arm, kind of twist and pull . . ."

Francis saw the livery and the freight yards ahead and kneed his horse into a trot before Lottie drove him into *wanting* to be hanged.

A sergeant met them. He had no neck, as near as Francis could tell, and was pouring sweat, though it was barely above freezing.

"We're here to be provisioned," Francis said. The sergeant hesitated until Francis told him that Lieutenant Brannigan had said it was all right.

"Fine, lad. You should have said so in the first place. There's grain in those bags, and bacon, and flour; beans and dried beef in that shed over there. Help yourself to what you'll be needing."

Francis took him at his word and loaded the mule down with sacks of flour, bacon, sugar, beans, and close to thirty pounds of oats for the stock. He also took several boxes of matches, two pounds of black powder, three tins of caps and a couple of five-pound pigs of lead. He had a mold and ladle to make rifle balls, but finding lead and powder was always a problem.

The mule didn't seem to mind the extra load, and they set off with perhaps another hour of daylight left, Francis feeling positively rich.

We're moving about four miles an hour, Francis thought, sitting on the walking horse. It was a mind game he played constantly. He factored in the speed and would look ahead to where he would be in an hour, see what was there to help him or hurt him.

In an hour we'll be by that ridge on the left. There are some thick trees along the base. Maybe there's water there. If not we can make a dry camp for the night. We have two canteens, and the animals can go a day more without water since the weather is cold.

Just thoughts rumbling through his mind all the time, information about his surroundings and what to expect. Sometimes he felt like a wolf. He'd watched them hunt several times and they didn't miss anything—they heard, saw, smelled everything around them. They'd stop and eat a mouse, a bug, a rabbit or a deer, then move around a rattlesnake—they just *knew* what was nearby. He tried to do the same, and to be alert, to not miss anything, and so was utterly surprised when the Mexican found them.

Chapter Six

They discovered a small stream. Francis suspected that it was dry most of the year, but with the snow in the mountains feeding it, there was a flow of water about five feet across, running through the trees and rippling over rocks.

They unsaddled and watered the horse and mule, gave them each about a quart of grain. Francis had some concern about giving them too much grain; they hadn't been fed anything but grass in so long he felt that they might founder on grain—but a small amount would certainly keep them in shape.

When they were fed he rubbed them down with the back side of the saddle blankets, inspected them for any sores or rubs, and then went to the camp.

Over the months the three travelers had become a team. As soon as they stopped Lottie picked a campsite and started a fire, and unpacked their tin plates and cups; Billy started gathering the large pile of wood it took to cook a meal and get them through a night—especially a cold night.

As soon as the fire was going well, Lottie put the large cast-iron pot onto the coals and started cooking. They had no game tonight, so she sliced bacon and put it in to fry, and used a second pot to start water boiling for "coffee." They didn't have any real coffee, but she would heat the water and sprinkle dry pine needles in it to make a kind of tea. When they had sugar, as they did now, they would sit after the meal and drink sweetened "tea."

Francis took his rifle and moved out away from the fire for a time. He circled, looking for tracks in the dying light—human or game—and sat off fifty yards under a *piñon* tree, hidden in the shadows for more than half an hour, waiting for something to move. When nothing seemed to be there he walked silently back to the campsite. Lottie had set the finished bacon on a tin plate and was cooking a kind of cornmeal mush in water and the bacon fat that was left in the pot. When it had thickened enough to "hold a spoon" she ladled it and three pieces of bacon on each plate, poured "tea" into each cup along with generous helpings of sugar, and set them by the fire. "Food's done."

They ate in silence—even Lottie—although she started to talk while they were sipping the tea. In the evenings Francis didn't mind her talking, for it was nice, almost a kind of music. He leaned back on his blankets, feeling the warmth of the fire and hearing every fifth word or so. His face ached where the ball had grazed him.

"I honestly don't understand why everybody gets in such a snit over land as to fight a war. I mean look at all this land around us that nobody is using. There's no need to fight. Just take some that isn't being used and get to living . . ."

It was difficult to stay awake. Finally, after throwing more wood on the fire, he rolled himself into his blankets and closed his eyes. Billy was already asleep and within a minute, while Lottie was still talking, Francis slept too.

FRANCIS WASN'T SURE what had awakened him: a sound, or the absence of it. Perhaps a chill. He opened his eyes to see a man wearing a *serape* squatting across the dead fire from him. The man smiled when he saw Francis's eyes open.

"*Hola, amigo.*" He said it softly and did not awaken Lottie or Billy.

Francis didn't speak. He felt for his rifle. It was still there. The man didn't appear to be armed—at least he couldn't see any weapons—but still, he was there. Francis sat up.

"How did you get here?" It was the second time Francis had been surprised on awakening. The first time had been when two men named Courtweiler and Dubs had come upon him and taken everything he owned. Nowadays Francis slept lightly, and he wondered that the horse or mule hadn't made a sound. "Without me knowing . . ."

"I followed you. And I am quiet," the man said in English. Not perfect, but better than many Americans. "It was not hard to track three children, a horse and a mule."

"Two children."

"Ahhh yes, there is that. You are now a man. A young man, but a man. You have killed another."

Francis looked to the fire. There were still a few coals faintly glowing; he put some twigs on them and blew them into flames. He added wood. In the dark it had been hard to see the man. Now Francis studied him in the light. He had a revolver on his belt, partially hidden beneath the *serape*. It glinted now. The man's hand was not near the butt of the gun; but still, the gun was there.

"Why are you here?"

"So blunt, the Americans. That is not the Spanish way. We should have talk and work up to the reason. First, we must introduce ourselves. I am García."

"I am—"

"I know who you are. That is why I am here. You are the man who shot and killed the American soldier yesterday."

"It was an accident. Or almost. I didn't mean to shoot him—"

"You do not understand. I am not angry. I am grateful. The woman you saved was Carmela. She is Garza's wife. Garza is my brother. I am here to help you because Garza has a dizziness in his head from his wound, so he could not come himself."

"Well, thank you. But I don't need any help."

García smiled and looked at the flames for a moment. "You do not need help. So confident. So young." He looked again at Francis. "You are very rich. You have a horse and a mule and food and a rifle and two children who have value, and so you have much wealth. You are traveling through a country that is very poor. There are some who would simply take what you have. Garza has asked that I accompany you for a time until you learn our ways and can take care of yourself . . ."

"But we're doing good."

"No, you're not. You think you are but you need guidance and I will provide it. If I do anything less Garza will be disappointed. A disappointed Garza is an angry Garza, and an angry Garza is . . . well, let us say it is not good when he is angered."

Francis thought and decided García was telling the truth. If he had wanted to steal anything he could have cut Francis's throat and been done with it. Francis nodded. "Well, as easy as you sneaked up on me, I guess you're right. I need the help. Go bring your horse in and tie him with ours. There's some grain in a sack by the packsaddle."

"I do not have a horse."

"Well, mule, whatever."

"I am on foot."

Francis shook his head. "With us riding and you on foot I don't see how you'll be able to keep up."

"I will stay ahead of you. That way I will know what is coming."

Francis leaned back on his blanket and smiled. He had started to say that García couldn't hope to keep up with people on horses but then remembered that he himself had caught up with Courtweiler and Dubs on foot when they had been riding.

"Let us sleep now," García said. "There are still three hours of darkness for resting. I will be over by the horse and mule if you need me."

And he was gone. Francis had done no more than blink, and when he looked again, García had disappeared.

A ghost, Francis thought. He hadn't even awakened the children. Just there and gone—I'm sure glad he's on our side. Francis closed his eyes and let the warmth of his blankets and the glow from the fire take him back down again.

Chapter Seven

The country they moved through the next day was in some strange way the prettiest country that Francis had ever seen. They moved down into a winding canyon that ran along the Rio Grande river, which went from cascading through narrow clifflike rocks to spreading wider and rolling through gentle rapids.

It was still desert, or near-desert, with scrub *piñon* and juniper and odd stands of prickly pear cactus, but the nearness of water made the desert seem more beautiful. When they came into a shallow valley full of small farms on narrow tracts of land with irrigation ditches running across the ends, it all looked like a picture.

"Ma, she had a calendar with a picture on it looked like these farms," Lottie started. "All set so nice and neat . . ."

Francis had seen the farms and the river moving through them, but he had been spending most of his time watching García. It was amazing. The Mexican carried a small bedroll over his shoulder and had his revolver—a Colt cap and ball—in his right hand. He ran in a kind of loose shuffle that left the horse and mule trotting to keep up. Since trotting was so uncomfortable that Francis and the children didn't want to do it, Francis kept the stock at a walk, and García, as he'd said, quickly left them far behind.

García had not been there when they had awakened in the morning and had not showed himself until they were two miles along the road. The first Lottie knew of him was when he stepped softly out of some *piñon* along the trail next to the mule.

"Hola, señorita," he said to her. For once she was speechless. "A very good morning to you . . ."

"Francis!" Lottie called ahead to where Francis was riding. "There's a strange man here."

"He's not strange," Francis said without turning. "Lottie and Billy, meet García. García, meet Lottie and Billy . . ."

"Where did he come from?" Lottie asked. "You have friends I don't know about out here? I don't think that's right . . ."

"He just showed up. A brother of the man where I had to shoot the soldier. He's here to help us, guide us."

"When did you meet him?"

"He came last night while you were sleeping. If you didn't sleep so hard you'd know these things. I tried to wake you, shook you, poured water on your head, but you were out like a light. I've never seen anybody sleep so hard. I thought you'd died. I woke Billy up and he tried to get you awake too and you wouldn't—"

"Stop that. You're just making up stories."

But it quieted her and Francis used the silence to talk to García. "I saw tracks," he said to García. The Mexican had moved up alongside Francis, holding onto the stirrup on the left side of his saddle and letting himself be pulled along.

Francis had seen a wide band of tracks come in

from the south side onto the road. They were all unshod horses and he couldn't tell for certain how many but he thought more than ten. They moved out ahead of the direction in which Francis and the children were traveling, and they were fresh. Some of the dirt cut by their hooves still looked damp in the morning cold and hadn't frozen.

"I have seen the same. There are many horses. Seven, perhaps ten, it is hard to tell when they all run together."

"They aren't army."

"No, the army horses have steel shoes. These have nothing."

"What do you think?"

García frowned, a quick flicker of concern. "I think it is perhaps not good. Nobody of any worth would be out riding around with seven or ten men on horses. If they aren't army then they must be somebody else and a group of men that large is usually up to no good."

"They're out ahead of us."

García nodded. "I will move off the trail and catch up to them and see. Keep moving but go slower and I will be back to you when I find out more." He slid off into the *piñon* and was gone, and Francis checked the percussion cap on his rifle, cleared a bit of dust off the front and rear sights, and wished he knew more about the tracks.

"What was that all about?" Lottie had seen them talking but hadn't heard what they said.

"García asked if I wanted him to find a good place to camp tonight and I said yes. He's gone ahead to locate water."

"Hmmm."

She didn't believe Francis but that didn't matter to him. He couldn't shake the feeling of worry about the tracks and had just decided to obey his instincts and stop altogether when the sound of gunfire came from ahead.

One shot, then two, then a whole ripping tear of them, and then nothing for a moment; then one more. Then silence. All in the space of four or five seconds.

It had to be García and he had to be in trouble. "Take Billy off the trail and head back up into the trees and hide," Francis said.

"Where are you going?"

"Just move! I'll be back . . ."

He kicked his horse in the ribs and slammed her into an instant gallop. It couldn't be far. García hadn't been gone that long. By her fourth jump he had taken three lead balls out of his possibles

bag and put them into his mouth, took three percussion caps and stuck them between the fingers on his left hand and brought the rifle up to be
ready.

It wasn't enough.

Chapter Eight

For a moment Francis thought he'd ridden into his own private war.

He came around a corner in the trail, the mare running wide open, his rifle ready, and found himself in the middle of what proved to be twelve men on horses.

Francis had flashes of images. Somehow all twelve men looked dirty at once, covered with trail dust, all riding scruffy Indian-style ponies—wild stock, very small and very tough—and all wore what he thought of as mixed Indian clothing. Leather leggings; wool blankets with holes cut for their heads; some had feathers, some wore old felt hats; some had no shirts on at all in spite of the cold. They were all covered in weapons. All had rifles or shotguns; some had bows and quivers full of arrows tied to their backs; others had one, two, even three revolvers in their belts. Francis saw tomahawks in belts. They were all shooting into the brush on the left side of the trail.

García, Francis thought; they must be shooting at García in there. And then a second thought: I have made a terrible mistake. There was no time for any other thought. He raised and cocked his rifle and picked a target. But before he could pull the trigger, what looked like all the guns in the world seemed to be aimed at him and they all fired at the same time.

He had time to see one ball crease the mare's neck, another nick her ear, and then something slammed into the side of his head and he had nothing resembling thought after that.

HE WAS SURE he was dead. There had been times before when he thought he would die—several times—but this time he was certain, and so when there seemed to be things happening in his mind, he thought he was either in heaven or hell. And whichever it was, Lottie's voice was there.

"I think it's disgraceful the way you just tied him up and dumped him across a saddle like a piece of meat. His head is all bloody, and I think I see his brains in there ready to leak out, and you're just letting him hang like that where they could flop out in the dirt . . ."

It all faded then into a kind of redness that covered him and he stayed that way until something jerked at him, pulled him sideways and threw him down to the ground.

"He might be dead already, for all you care. Look at him, he's all shot to pieces. What's he going to be worth to you if his brains flop out?"

This time Francis tried opening his eyes. He was on his back, and when he opened them the sun was shining directly into them and seemed to shoot a hot spear into the center of his head. He jerked his eyes shut. It did not stop Lottie's voice.

"Where are you taking us? All I see ahead is mountains and brush. Nobody of a civil nature would take two children into a wilderness—ummph!" There was a thump and Lottie's voice stopped. This time Francis turned away from the sun a bit and opened his eyes and kept them open.

His head was exploding in pain; waves of it came from the left side over to the right. He started to reach up and feel it but his hands were tied together. When he tried to roll and free his arms, somebody in back kicked him in the ribs hard enough to make the breath whistle out of his nose.

He lay still on his side and tried to focus on what he could see. A forest of horses' legs was there, standing still. There was a smell of horse sweat, so they had been working hard. Men moved back and forth tightening cinches and checking hooves. They were stopped in a small clearing in a stand of *piñon* and juniper. The ground was rocky. He could not see Lottie or Billy or García without moving, and he was afraid that if he moved, the men would kick him again and he would pass out. It had all come back to him now, riding into the men, raising his rifle, getting shot at. García. What had happened to García? Probably dead.

Aside from the pain in his head and what he thought was dried blood caked there and down the side of his face, he had another burning pain across his left thigh. It looked like a ball had creased there, only slightly breaking the skin. That must be the problem with his head as well: A ball had creased him. How in heaven's name could all those men shoot at him and miss? And after not killing him in the first place, why did they keep him alive and not just shoot him and be done with it?

"Up," somebody said in English and kicked Francis again, this time in the back.

Francis rolled onto his stomach, worked his knees beneath him and levered himself up. His head was on fire. He didn't move fast enough and somebody kicked him again.

"Francis, you have to get up and get on a horse. These men will shoot you sure if you can't ride." Lottie's voice sounded on the edge of crying. "Please get up . . ."

"Lottie?"

"Shut up!" Another kick, but this time the force of the blow helped him move up and he gained his feet. "Mount."

There was the mare standing next to him. She had a bloodied ear and blood down her neck from the wound there but was apparently not hit in any other place. It was a miracle, he thought—that he hadn't been riddled and that somehow they hadn't hit the mare solid either.

He grabbed the saddle horn and pulled himself

up, foot in the stirrup, leg up and over, sitting there, on the edge of vomiting with pain but sitting there hanging on to the horn with his tied hands and weaving slightly.

Now he could see better as well.

They had been climbing into a shallow pass, heading south by the direction the sun stood. He had been facedown over the saddle; his stomach was bruised, and his shoulders and arms were sore from bumping against the side of the horse. How long he had been unconscious he couldn't guess.

The men worked on in silence. They were, now that Francis had had time to study them, very hard men. Some of them looked to be full-blood Indians and some appeared to be mixed, but they all knew horses and wasted no time checking their mounts. There was no water but some snow in patches. They rubbed the snow up inside their horses' lips to moisten them. They had ridden hard, Francis thought, and planned to ride harder.

Lottie and Billy were still on the mule ahead of him three or four paces, Lottie looking back with worry in her eyes. She had a bruise on the side of her face where she'd been struck. Billy had been crying but he seemed quiet now and was looking at the men the way Francis had studied them—checking their gear, their mounts, the way they looked. Francis almost smiled. Billy was growing faster than he'd thought.

He started to say something but Lottie saw his face and shook her head, held her finger to her lips and whispered, "They don't like it if you talk."

"Shut up," a man mounted next to her said. "Or we will leave you tied to a tree for the coyotes . . ."

There was no chance for talk after that. The men mounted, spread out in single file with Francis on the mare and Lottie and Billy on the mule in the middle and set off without speaking another word.

Headed south. Away from any civilization, away from the trail west, away from help.

Away.

Chapter Nine

Francis had done some long riding in his time, hard riding and hard living, but he had never experienced anything like what these men did now. He didn't think men could stand it. Even more, he didn't think horses could take it.

They simply didn't stop.

As the day wore on Francis felt the pain diminishing to a steady throb that kept the side of his head burning. The dizziness left him, and he worked his wrists to loosen the tie there so that his blood would circulate better. In spite of her wounds, the mare kept up the pace easily—she was, like the others, a tamed wild horse and had enormous stamina. The mule kept up as well.

Billy stuck to the packsaddle like a burr but Lottie started to have trouble toward the end of the day. She weaved and Francis would see her catch herself to keep from falling asleep and falling off the mule.

In late afternoon, they stopped but not to rest. The men all dismounted and made Francis and the children do the same. Francis thought they would stop for the night but he was wrong. They loosened the cinches on the horses for no more than five minutes, retightened them and remounted.

They can't be serious, Francis thought. They're not going to keep riding. One of the men dug into his saddlebags and handed each of the children and Francis a piece of jerky.

"Eat."

"But I'm thirsty," Lottie said. "And Billy is too . . ."

The man struck her once alongside the head. "Eat."

She started to chew the jerky, and Billy did the same. Francis did likewise and within moments they were riding again.

At first Francis had the strength to think while

they rode. The men were running—he was sure of it. Initially he thought they were Indians but some of them spoke Spanish and several spoke English fairly well, and they didn't seem to be of a tribe. Renegades, he thought.

Afternoon bled into evening and soon it grew dark and cold. The men didn't care. The leader kept the pace, riding somewhere ahead in the darkness. The rest followed with Francis and the children in the middle.

They came out of the mountains in the darkness and started riding across flat prairie. The stars were brilliant enough to give some light, and when a sliver of moon came up it seemed almost daylight.

All night they rode. Just before dawn, when it was coldest, the leader stopped and dismounted and the rest of them did the same. Francis thought surely they will stop now; surely they have run far enough to be safe.

But they did not. The men jumped around and slapped their arms against their sides to get warm. They let the children take care of their "personal business," as Lottie called it, gave them another piece of jerky and a short swallow from a canteen, and retightened cinches before remounting and setting the same crippling pace.

The sun crawled up and by this time Francis was

on the edge of hallucinating. He kept seeing shadows jumping out at the edge of his vision. Billy was fast asleep, somehow maintaining his balance, and Lottie had jammed herself into the packsaddle and was sleeping as well.

It was then, just before the sun was high enough to provide warmth, that Francis found out who had them.

The men hardly spoke, and when they felt it necessary they kept it low, just above a whisper. But as Francis dozed the mare moved ahead a bit to be near two of them and one of them said the word: "Comanche."

Francis's eyes snapped open and he knew instantly who they were. Not Indians, not Comanches—these men were Comancheros.

Francis had heard stories of the Comanches down south—mostly in Texas. They were universally feared and made raids for plunder and prisoners as far as the northern edge of the Texas frontier.

From what he'd heard, they were bad enough. But worse were the dreaded Comancheros, groups of men who traded with the Comanches. It would explain how they worked the horses. At one of the trading posts, Francis had heard mountain men talking of the Comancheros and how they rode.

They said a white man could drive a horse until it dropped, then a Comanche could get the horse up and get forty more miles out of it before it dropped again, but a Comanchero could come along, get two hundred more miles out of it, then eat it when it finally collapsed. Tough men.

When they had stolen stock and goods from raiding, the Comanches would meet bands of Comancheros to trade for ammunition, weapons, flour, sugar, lead, and salt. Sometimes, Francis had heard, the Comanches would keep children to raise as slaves.

The Comancheros had a reputation worse than the Comanches themselves. As near as Francis could figure it, he and the children were being taken by a band of them down into the south country where the Comanches roamed.

Absolutely nothing good could come from it. They would be sold, he thought. Or worse: separated and given to the Comanches.

There was only one way open for them. They had to escape.

But the Comancheros kept driving south, farther and farther away from any possible help, into a country Francis did not know. With every step escape seemed more and more impossible. If they would just stop, Francis thought, give him time to think, to rest.

But the pace never let up. They ate riding, slept riding, and kept moving, somehow keeping the horses going by force of will.

All day they moved, stopping only once to loosen and retighten cinches, to take a sip of water and a bite of jerky. All day and into the night they kept riding until Francis felt like he'd never done anything else; moving until Lottie and Billy became part of the mule and packsaddle. All through the night and into the next day. Finally, out in the flats of the prairie, they came upon a cut, a wide canyon that didn't show until they were almost on top of it.

The leader led them down a winding trail wide enough for one horse along the canyon wall. Far below Francis could see a group of small shacks in a stand of cottonwoods—little more than brush huts covered with skins—and a winding stream. It was too far away to see any people, but he could make out a fairly large herd of horses, and by squinting, he finally saw small figures running back and forth. Some wagons were parked near the shacks. As they dropped down the canyon wall, Francis could hear dogs barking.

It wasn't a village so much as a mobile camp, and if this trail was the only way out, it didn't leave much hope for escape. Not that it mattered so much now. Francis was so tired he couldn't make his brain work to formulate a plan anyway; so tired he had difficulty paying attention to anything but keeping his balance on the mare.

She was tired as well. When they came out into the bottom of the canyon, she began to weave and wobble and he knew she would go down soon. She somehow stayed on her feet until they were near the horse herd, then she settled gently to the ground. Francis stepped off as she caved in, and as if she were signaling, half the other horses went down as well.

The men dismounted and unsaddled, dragging gear off the horses without making them rise. Some other men and a few women—as dirty as the men who had taken them prisoner—came out and greeted them, all without talking except in low murmurs. They spoke a mixture of Indian dialect and Spanish as they helped to strip gear off the horses and drag it to the wagons.

A woman came over to Lottie and pinched her cheek. Lottie kicked her and the woman backhanded the girl, slapping her so hard that Francis heard her teeth click.

"Leave me alone!" Lottie was half asleep on her feet. "Just leave me—"

The woman grabbed her hand and took Billy's as well—he was standing near Lottie, his eyes closed—and dragged them into one of the huts.

"Where are you taking them?" Francis started after them without thinking. One of the men stepped up in back of him and quietly, professionally thumped Francis just under his left ear with the brass butt of his rifle.

Francis went down like a stone.

Chapter Ten

"Francis! Wake up, Francis! We need you—you have to wake up!"

Lottie's voice, insistent, pushing, pulling him awake. He opened his eyes and saw a dark brush ceiling over him. Then Lottie's face came into view, and next to her, Billy's. Billy was chewing on a piece of jerky.

"What . . ."

"One of them hit you on the back of the head with his gun. Billy and I dragged you in here—the woman let us—and then they went away and they haven't been back, and I untied your hands. I think they're expecting somebody because they killed one of the horses and are cutting it up to roast. I've been watching them through a crack in the wall. It's not hard. The wall is all cracks. There isn't actually a wall at all, just a bunch of sticks you could throw a cat through—"

"Lottie, please. Quiet. My head is killing me and I have to think. I know who they are now."

"So do I. They're called Comancheros. I heard some of them talking and they used the word. Is that a bad thing? I mean I know it can't really be good, the way they're treating us and all. But are Comancheros really awful, like I think?"

Francis shut his eyes. "As bad as it gets, from what I hear. We have to get out of here."

"Not until we get some rest. Billy fell asleep standing up and I'm near ready to drop."

"All right. One of us should stay awake and watch them. I rested some on the mare so I'll take the first watch— Oh, she's not the horse they killed to eat, is she?"

"No. It was a scruffy wild thing they had in the herd."

"Good. I've been through a lot with that mare . . ."

Lottie had settled against the wall. She seemed

to shrink into her blanket pullover and was asleep instantly.

Francis sat and leaned back against the other side of the hut, and turned so that he could see between the branches.

There wasn't much happening. The men who had taken them prisoner were asleep as well, and some older men and women—there were no children—were dragging in wood and making large fires. Francis could see the dead horse where they'd shot it. Two women were cutting chunks of meat from it, hanging them over sticks near the fire.

There were half a dozen mangy dogs nearby. They clearly wanted the meat but stayed away from it out of fear. Francis saw why when one of them came a little too close and a woman hit it with a piece of firewood so hard that it ran off screaming, dragging a leg.

Nice, Francis thought. Really nice people here, these Comancheros.

He dozed. Every part of him hurt: his hips and legs from riding, his head from the bullet strike and the rifle butt, his arms from being tied. He didn't sleep but he dozed, in and out, catching himself when his head dropped and snapping his eyes open. But at last he couldn't stay awake.

He wasn't sure how long he'd slept—several hours—and it was dark when he awoke. Lottie and Billy were still asleep, and he wondered for a moment what had awakened him. Then he heard it. Men and women were running back and forth, dogs were barking in alarm.

Somebody was coming and Francis moved to the doorway of the hut to see.

It was pitch dark, the lowering sky threatening to snow. Aside from the fire there was almost no light.

The dogs were all barking toward the northeast and Francis watched that direction until he saw a figure looming out of the darkness. One man on a horse, pulling two other packhorses with huge loads piled so high that the horses looked like dwarf ponies.

But it was the man who caught his eye.

The man sat straight in the saddle and was wearing a buffalo robe for warmth. He had a rifle balanced across his lap, though he didn't seem concerned that he might be in danger, and the rifle just lay there cradled. The packhorses followed him naturally—he didn't have a rope back to them—and as he rode near the fire he raised his right hand in greeting and smiled. His left arm was missing and he was wearing a derby-style hat with a feather in it.

"No," Francis said half aloud. "It can't be . . ."

The man sitting on his horse by the fire, greeting the Comancheros like old friends, was Jason Grimes.

— Chapter Eleven —

Francis was stunned. Memories roared back. His capture by the Pawnees, Grimes "helping" him escape, their life together trapping until Grimes fought a man named Braid in single-handed combat. Grimes had reverted into a kind of madness as he mutilated the dead Braid.

Grimes had been badly wounded in that fight, and Francis had struck out on his own, angry at Grimes for becoming what he considered so evil. He'd thought it probable that the mountain man had died of his injuries.

Clearly he had survived. And just as clearly he was not trapping beaver any longer. He had become a businessman, judging by the enormous loads on the two packhorses. A trader.

Somebody who traded with the Comancheros.

Talk about stooping low, Francis thought, watching Grimes and the men unpack the horses near the fire. Grimes could crawl under a snake.

"Who is it?" Lottie had awakened and was peering through the brush wall next to Francis. "You *know* him? Is that *another* friend?"

"Not a friend, exactly. He was, but I don't know what he is now."

"Will he help us escape?"

Francis frowned. "I don't know. He helped me get away from the Pawnees once but things were different then. Now . . ."

Lottie sighed. "I hope he will, Francis. I'm ever so worried about us."

"Me too, Lottie. Don't worry, I'll think of something."

The problem was that Francis *had* been trying to think of a way out but it looked impossible. Alone he could cut and run and might have a chance. But with the two children—and there was absolutely no way he would leave without them—it became much more difficult. They slowed him down and there was the added responsibility of having them near; he couldn't take foolish risks that might endanger them.

They had added wood to the fire outside and Grimes was showing his goods to trade, as he had done with the Pawnees. He had powder and lead, but he also had some mirrors and blankets and sugar; some cheap knives and tomahawks; and dried apples, other dried fruit, and some salt. He passed blankets and bolts of material around, spread one blanket on the ground and displayed his wares there. They soon had a brisk trade going. The Co-mancheros needed the goods to trade with the Comanches when they came. In return they gave Grimes pelts and cash money the Indians had given them previously.

Francis watched all this and wondered how he could get Grimes's attention. If the mountain man couldn't help him escape, maybe he could do something for the children.

As the trading grew more excited, squabbles broke out over items that several people wanted. Two men wanted the same blanket, and they soon pulled knives out and went at it. One man— larger than the rest, the man who had led the raiding party that had taken Francis and the children—held up his hand and stopped the trading.

He said something in broken English to Grimes and pointed to the brush hut where Francis stood watching.

Grimes shook his head and motioned for the trading to continue. The leader made a "No" sign and pointed again at the hut. Finally Grimes stood and walked in the direction of the captives.

The leader grabbed a burning stick off the fire and followed. He stopped at the door of the hut and held the torch up so that Grimes could see in.

"Pasqual, there ain't nothing in here but a couple of pups. I ain't going to give you my whole poke for a couple of sprites. What would I want with pups?"

"Hello." Francis took a step away from the wall into the light. "How are you doing, Mr. Grimes?"

For a full three seconds, the mountain man stood still. Then he took the torch from the Comanchero and held it out.

"Mr. Tucket—is that you?"

Francis nodded.

"Why, I thought you went on west to join them farmers you missed . . ."

"I got sidetracked."

Grimes looked at the children. "I should say so—are these your kin?"

"In a way."

"You wouldn't consider leaving them?"

"No."

"It was a stupid question, knowing you and how much you like the niceties of civilization."

"I don't believe in hacking up dead bodies, if that's what you mean."

"It don't seem like you're in a position to be picking at people . . ."

"I'm sorry. It just slipped out." And as Francis said it, he realized he meant it—he *was* sorry. In a way, he was genuinely glad to see the mountain man, and not just because he hoped to get help. Seeing him now, he felt that he'd missed him. "I'm sorry . . ."

Grimes was silent for a time, the fire from the torch flickering on his face. Then he sighed. "You sure do cause me a peck of trouble."

"I didn't mean to."

"The way the stick floats is me and this Pasqual are friends, ain't we, Pasqual?"

The man nodded, smiling through broken teeth. *"Amigos, sí . . ."*

"He don't understand a whole bunch of English so we can talk a bit. We're friends, but the friendship is on account of what I can bring them when I come trading. If I don't bring them anything my hair will probably go to a Comanche in trade—"

"So you have all that stuff on the packhorses," Lottie cut in. "Give him that."

"Speaks right up, don't she?" Grimes looked at Francis.

Francis nodded. "She doesn't hold back much."

"The problem is this Pasqual is a heap good trader. He wants to keep his gold *and* get the trade goods."

"Ahhh . . ."

Grimes nodded. "So he told me he'd trade all three of you for what I've got and we'd call her square."

"Sounds like a good deal to me," Lottie whispered.

"The tight part is all I own is wrapped up in these goods. I trade for you and I wind up with nothing to keep going."

"I'll pay you back," Francis said. "Somehow. I'll get work and pay you back."

Grimes nodded. "Yes, Mr. Tucket. That would be one way to handle it. And I know you'd hold to it. But I'm about done trading with these yahoos anyway, and I thought there might be another way to make a poke."

Francis waited. The torch had burned down to a small flicker, about the size of a candle flame, and Pasqual took it and swore when it burned his fingers. He dropped it in the dirt.

"Remember when we dealt with them Pawnees?" Grimes spoke out of the sudden darkness.

"Pawnees?" Francis said.

"You know, when you visited them Pawnees for a while and then I came and we met there. Remember how that went?"

"Ohhh. Sure." Francis had been a captive and Grimes had "arranged" for a horse to be ready for him if he got away. "It's a little more complicated now, what with my new family."

"I figured that. Just remember how all that happened and we'll work it the same way now. I'll go trade with Pasqual and we'll open a barrel of trade whiskey and see what happens later."

"Later," Francis repeated.

"Ayup. You just keep your powder dry and keep this little missy quiet, and I'm going to go have me a shindig with Pasqual."

And he left the hut and went back to the fire.

"What did he mean?" Lottie asked. "All that

talking around the corners of things—what did he mean?"

"He meant," Francis said, settling down with his back to the wall, "that we aren't going to get a lot of rest tonight."

Chapter Twelve

In spite of what he had said, Francis made Lottie and Billy sleep, or at least try to. The idea of escaping with Grimes made him think of the situation and what they were up against. He could not forget the ride here—the endlessness of it, the way the men kept on going and never quit.

How they could get away from these same men posed a problem that Francis needed to think about. Grimes might be able to set something up, but that didn't mean it would succeed.

If the Comancheros chased as hard as they ran, it would be next to impossible to get away with Lottie and Billy. The mare was done and the mule was not much better, which meant they would have to take different horses from the Comanchero herd. What if they didn't get good stock? What if they didn't get away? What would the Comancheros do to them if they tried to run and failed?

What if . . .

He finally stopped thinking about it. There were too many variables to make any kind of prediction—so much that could go wrong. It came down to a very simple, possibly deadly problem. One: They couldn't stay and get traded to the Comanches. Two: The Comancheros wouldn't let them go voluntarily. Three: They had to run.

Whether they made it or not, they still had to run, had to try, and that was that.

Lottie and Billy finally slept. The temperature had warmed slightly, and they seemed comfortable enough in their blanket pullovers. Francis sat by the wall and watched the celebration through the brushy wall of the hut. Grimes had broken open the top of a small keg of whiskey. He dipped tin cups in the brew and handed them to the men around the fire, and in a very short time they were all as drunk as Francis had ever seen—with the possible exception of the army commandant.

They did not stop the party because they were drunk but kept on until the barrel was empty. Then Mr. Grimes started trading. He pointed at the hut where the children were and shook his head and waved his hands. He didn't want the children. He wanted gold. He would trade for gold. And soon, lubricated by the whiskey, the Comancheros started bringing out gold they had gotten from Comanche trading. And by the time they were all nearly drunk enough to pass out, Grimes had sold all his goods and had a small sack of gold coins.

He had been drinking with the men, taking the cup on each pass. Could Grimes help them escape if he was drunk?

The mountain man was soon weaving and wobbling as much as the Comancheros, and when most of the men left and returned to their huts—falling all over themselves—Grimes was as drunk as the rest. He fell back on his blanket by the fire, rolled up and passed out. The few remaining Comancheros tried to scoop more whiskey out of the empty keg and then drifted off.

And that, Francis thought, watching it all, was that. So much for running. He turned away and settled his back against the side of the hut, his mind full of bitter thoughts. How could it have been any different? Grimes was still Grimes—a rough man in the company of other rough men. Why would he risk it all just to save three kids—one of whom he didn't even like?

Francis let his eyes close, opened them and checked Grimes once more. When he saw that the mountain man was still unconscious, he closed them again. Not to sleep, he thought—just to rest and be ready for what would come the next day. Just a moment . . .

"Were you going to sleep all night, Mr. Tucket?"

Francis opened his eyes slowly to find Mr. Grimes standing in front of him in the darkness of the hut. "I thought you were drunk and I must have fallen asleep . . ."

"I was letting on. It takes a heap to make me drunk even when I'm drinking and I wasn't drinking. And you were supposed to be ready . . ."

"I am."

"Get the sprites up. We have to move *now*." And Grimes disappeared into the darkness.

Francis shook Lottie and Billy. Lottie snapped awake instantly, but Billy took a moment.

"Come on—there's no time to waste. You take my hand and hang on to Billy's with your other one. We don't want to get separated in the dark. Do exactly as I tell you and be quiet."

Francis moved out of the hut. Grimes hadn't said where he was going because he hadn't needed to. They needed horses and that meant the horse herd at the edge of the encampment. Francis dragged the two children at a dead run.

Grimes was already there with his three horses. One was saddled and the other two had packsaddles on them.

He whispered, "You'll have to ride the packhorses. Most of their stock seems awful rundown."

"We rode hard getting here. They haven't rested enough yet." Francis thought briefly of the mare and the mule. He hated to leave them, but they hadn't recovered enough.

"No more talk. We have to ride. Throw the pups up on one horse and you take the other."

When Francis got close to the packhorses, he

saw that they had some gear tied to their saddles. His rifle was there, along with his powder horn and possibles bag. "You got my gun!"

Grimes snorted. "I remembered it from before. Thought you might need it. The man who had it was so drunk he won't know it's gone for a week."

They moved through the horse herd, leading their mounts—Francis pulling the horse with Lottie and Billy on top. For a time, it seemed they would make it. They had cleared the herd and were twenty paces into dark prairie when a dog started barking.

Francis didn't know what set it off but as soon as it barked another joined it and soon every dog in the village was yelping.

It woke some of the drunk Comancheros, who yelled at the dogs. Grimes had stopped, frozen, waiting for the clamor to subside. It nearly did.

But one of the Comancheros was sick and wandered to the edge of the village to throw up no more than thirty feet from the little group.

At first he didn't see them. He finished his business and was turning away when something caught his eye—a flash of metal in the moonlight, the dark mass of a horse against the starry sky. Something.

"*¿Qué?*" He leaned forward, peering into the dark, and still almost didn't see them.

Then Billy sneezed.

"*Hooo!*"

It sounded like a whistle—a big owl hooting—but it got the job done. Drunk or not, the camp lived on the edge of danger every moment, and they came awake instantly with the alarm.

The man who had yelled didn't have a gun, but he had a belt knife. He pulled it and went for Grimes. The mountain man stepped to the side and clubbed him down with his rifle, then swung into the saddle. "We're for it now. Let's go."

And he wheeled and vanished into the darkness. Francis threw his leg up over the packhorse and followed, kicking the horse into speed although he didn't need to. The two packhorses were accustomed to following Grimes and they slammed out at a dead run.

It was hard to stay astride. The packsaddle was covered with a piece of folded empty canvas but it didn't have stirrups. Soon they were at a wild lope through darkness over broken ground and Francis had dropped the rope leading to the second packhorse. He wanted to check on Lottie and Billy but couldn't turn. He yelled back, "Are you with me?"

"With you? We're *ahead* of you!"

And they were. The packhorses had followed Grimes and his mount when the mountain man had taken off. The children's horse was faster than Francis's.

It was a miracle that they didn't fall. Grimes kept them at a hard run for well over an hour, until the horses were snorting and blowing, before he slowed them to a walk to catch their wind.

They had caught up to him and Grimes spoke while they rode. "We don't have much time before they catch us."

"With that ride?" Francis felt his horse heaving, trying to suck air.

"Don't forget who they are. We have the night helping us. They'll track slow in the dark and if we keep moving we might stretch it a bit, but they'll come on hard and we won't have much time."

"What can we do?" Lottie's face looked white in the darkness.

Grimes was quiet for a time, thinking. "I figure we've come twelve, fourteen miles. I know where we are. The river canyon lies just north of here—two, three miles. Maybe four. There's water and game there. You'll be able to hide, get food—"

"What are you saying here?" Francis cut in. "You're going to leave us?"

Grimes nodded. "It's the only way. They're after three horses. If you get off here and walk north and I keep moving west with the packhorses, they'll come after me. You cover your tracks and they won't see them in the dark. With light stock and no pups I can keep ahead of them for days, maybe forever. They'll think you're with me and it will give you time to get away north, get back to help."

"You're deserting us," Lottie said. "Of all the cold things to do . . ."

Francis had thought the same thing at first but now shook his head. "He's right, Lottie. If we stay with him we'll be slower and they'll catch us. It's the only way we have a chance. We have to separate." But still something held him and he thought a moment before he realized what it was—he didn't want to leave the mountain man. At one time he had never wanted to see Grimes again, but now he realized that he had missed Grimes a great deal.

"I don't want to leave you," he said and realized how it sounded: soft, silly. "I mean—"

"I know what you mean," Grimes said, his

voice low. "It was right good to see you again too, although I wish we could meet under some easier conditions. I'd like to ride with you awhile myself, but this is the only way."

"I know."

"And if we waste time jawing and palavering, they're going to ride up on us."

"I know."

"So dismount and go."

"Where are you going? Maybe we can meet up again." Francis swung off and held the second packhorse while the children jumped down; took his rifle and possibles sack; then handed the two lead ropes to Grimes.

"Straight west until I lose them, and then I'll start swinging north. I'll stay where it's warm for the winter because my bones are old and I don't like the cold like I once did. Look for me there. Where it's warm. Cover your tracks as you head north and keep your hair on and your powder dry."

And he was gone before Francis could think, I should have thanked him.

"I don't like him," Lottie said as he disappeared into the darkness.

"I didn't for a while. But I changed. He grows on you. Come on, we don't have time to talk."

As it happened they had less time than Francis had thought. He made the two children walk ahead of him in single file. Following them closely, he broke off a small branch of mesquite and brushed over their tracks as best he could in the dark as they moved.

In not more than ten minutes he heard hooves coming hard.

"Stop now," he whispered. Seeing the children's faces in the dark, Lottie's white and round, he added, "Turn away from the sound, lie down, and not a sound now, not a sound at all."

He actually saw the riders pass. It was too dark to count them—more than ten, maybe fifteen men—but they were pushing their horses and they thundered past the children not sixty yards away without seeing them.

They'll catch Grimes, he thought, watching them fade into the night. Moving that fast they'll come up on him before morning. He has just the one gun, and I should have stayed with him. We'd have taken two of them, maybe four before they took us . . .

Then he shook his head, remembering who Grimes was, what he'd done, how tough he was; he took some catching. If he was caught, he would take some holding. He smiled then and thought Grimes must have been something with two arms, hard as he was with only one. I hope I see him again.

"Come on," he whispered to the children, starting them moving north again, "we've got some ground to cover."

GARY PAULSEN is the distinguished author of many critically acclaimed books for young people, including three Newbery Honor books: *The Winter Room, Hatchet* and *Dogsong*. His novel *The Haymeadow* received the Western Writers of America Golden Spur Award. Among his newest Delacorte Press books are *Brian's Winter* (a companion to *Hatchet*), *Nightjohn, Call Me Francis Tucket* and *Father Water, Mother Woods: Essays on Fishing and Hunting in the North Woods*. He has also published fiction and nonfiction for adults. He and his wife have homes in New Mexico and on the Pacific coast.

When Francis Tucket is separated from his family and their wagon train as they head west along the Oregon Trail, he has only just turned fourteen. Will he survive the dangers that lie ahead of him? Will he ever find his family?

In *Mr. Tucket*, Francis meets the mountain man, Jason Grimes, who teaches him how to survive on his own. Francis continues his journey west in *Call Me Francis Tucket*. In this novel, Francis takes on the responsibility of caring for two orphans who join him as he moves toward new adventures.

Read more about the action-packed Western adventures of Francis Tucket in *Mr. Tucket* and *Call Me Francis Tucket* by Gary Paulsen.

DON'T MISS THE VERY FIRST
TUCKET ADVENTURE . . .

ISBN: 0-440-41133-5

"A real knock 'em, sock 'em ripsnorter
guaranteed to keep any boy and any girl . . .
enthralled from first page through last."
—*Publishers Weekly*

Now available from Yearling Books

—— Chapter Four ——

There are certain things that are always easy to remember because of the way they happen. Francis's first sight of Mr. Jason Grimes was like that. He would remember it always because of the way Mr. Grimes ignored the Pawnees. It was not an easy thing to do. The Indian dogs were snapping at the hooves of his horses and pack mules, and the squaws and children were so thick all around him that he only showed from the waist up. Yet he ignored them, threading his horse carefully, gracefully around the noisy women and children, looking off in space as though they didn't exist. He made quite a figure as he rode, straight backed, moving easily with the horse's roll. Francis got more of an impression of a piece of timber bolted to a saddle than a man—until he looked at Mr. Grimes's face. It was a thin face, and almost as dark as an Indian's, except that it bore a bushy beard and mustache. He had thin lips and washed-out blue eyes, and on top of his head he wore a dashing but dusty derby, set slightly back, with one long feather sticking straight up from the band. He had on fringed but otherwise not very fancy buckskins, plain moccasins, and no belt.

The last thing Francis noted was that Mr. Grimes's left arm was gone. He carried his rifle, wrapped in a buckskin case, with the same hand that loosely held his horse's reins, and the fact that he had no left arm didn't seem to bother him at all. It seemed almost natural, as though he would have looked odd *with* a left arm.

Francis realized suddenly that he was staring with his mouth open. He shut it. He moved forward through the crowd around the mountain man.

"Hey," he called. "Hey, over here. I'm a *captive*!" The word sounded funny when he said it, but he saw that the mountain man had heard, for he looked down from his horse quickly, then back up. Francis wasn't sure, but he thought the derby-topped head had shaken left to right just once—as though telling him to be quiet.

Then he couldn't see anything more because his "mother" found him and dropped a noose over his head. She dragged him back, cackling happily, and led him into a corner of the lodge.

With his hands tied in back of him and his ankles lashed firmly together, Francis had plenty of time to think. Most of his thoughts were about the mountain man. How could he come into the Pawnee camp and not be harmed? And *why* had he come? Was he a friend of the Indians?

There were no answers in that dark corner of the lodge, but one thing was plain. The Pawnee weren't going to kill the mountain man. Just the opposite—his arrival was to be the reason for a full day of celebrating. Francis heard all the preparations, and with this knowledge, his heart sank. Any man that friendly with the Pawnees wouldn't be likely to offer him help in escaping.

All that day he lay in the lodge, wondering. He got no food and no water. By nine that night, when the dancing had reached its full frenzy, he at last fell asleep.

Francis wasn't sure of the time when he opened

his eyes, but it was either very late that same night or very early the following morning. He did know why he had awakened. There was a calloused hand clamped over his mouth, and in the darkness of the lodge, he could make out the shape of a derby.

It was the mountain man.

Francis felt the bushy beard against his ear, and heard a whisper.

"Don't move. No sound. Just blink your eyes if you hear me and are wide awake."

Francis blinked, and the hand was taken off his mouth.

"Can you ride?" the mountain man asked, still whispering hoarsely.

Francis nodded.

"Good. In back of the lodge you'll find a little black mare I swiped from the Pawnee herd. Walk her out of camp with your hand over her muzzle. When you're safely out of camp, get on her and ride as hard as you can with the North Star on your right shoulder—" He stopped suddenly as Francis's "mother," across the lodge, turned in her sleep. In a second he continued, "If you ride hard enough, and don't hit a hole somewhere, dawn will catch you at a small creek. Take the mare right into the middle of the creek and head upstream. Keep going in the water until you think you're going to drop, then go another ten miles. If you stop, they'll get you. Now, did you understand all that?"

Francis nodded again, "Where will you be?" he asked, rubbing his wrists, which the mountain man had cut loose while he was talking.

"Why, I'll be sitting right here in camp," the mountain man answered, chuckling softly, "eating a good breakfast, wondering whether or not they've caught you. If they don't, I'll see you in a couple of days. Now, are you going to sit and jaw all night or get riding?"

Francis took it for the command it was. Thirty seconds later he was leading the little mare quietly out of the village, hoping with all his heart that he smelled enough like an Indian not to upset the dogs.

A minute after that he was on her back, wishing he'd never told a lie in his life. The only time he'd ever been on a horse was when he'd ridden a workhorse while his father plowed. That had only been at a walk, and with a lot of harness straps to hang on to.

The little black mare didn't even have a blanket on her back and she only had two speeds—dead stop and full run.

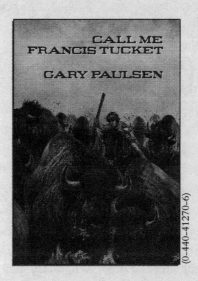

Chapter Three

"Ahh, see here, Dubs, what fate has provided for us . . . ," a deep, professorial-sounding voice boomed.

It was a dream, Francis was sure of it. It simply wasn't possible that a human voice could be speaking and for a full five seconds he refused to open his eyes and lose the relaxing comfort of sleep.

"Come now, lad. Don't be lazy. We have business afoot. Wake up."

Francis opened his eyes.

At first it didn't matter. The sun was full up and when his lids opened the brightness blinded him.

He blinked, let his eyes adjust, turned away from the sun and opened them again.

He was staring at the dead fire, or more accurately across the fire. There was a man sitting, squatting back on his haunches. He looked old to Francis, over forty, and was so heavily bearded Francis could not see his face for the hair.

But the clothing was more startling. The man was short, almost fat, and dressed in a black suit including a black vest, black boots, black trousers and black frock coat, and a full top hat on his head.

"See, Dubs, the lad awakens." The man smiled—his teeth broken and jagged; a bit of tobacco juice oozed out the side of the lip into the beard and the lines around his black eyes did not match the smile.

Francis slid his hand toward the rifle. Or where the rifle had been. He could not find it.

"See, Dubs, even now he reaches for his weapon. A true child of the frontier." The man spoke to somebody else—Francis couldn't see anybody at first—but kept looking at Francis. The smile widened. Like a snake getting ready to hiss. A hair snake. "I have your rifle—and a nice piece it is, too."

"What . . . who are you?" Francis at last found words. "What are you doing here?"

"Exactly!" The man nodded, waved a filthy finger. "That's exactly what *I* said, wasn't it, Dubs—when we came upon the lad, didn't I say just that? We came over the hill at dawn and I saw you sleeping there and saw your horse and I turned to Dubs and whispered—so as not to disturb your slumbers—and I said: Who is this, and what is he doing here?"

Francis sat up, or tried to. Something heavy, like warm iron, descended on his head and shoulders and pressed him back down. He swiveled his head back and saw that he was looking at a giant—a true giant. It was a man in crude buckskins, so large he seemed to blot out the sun, and Francis saw that the giant had put a hand down to keep him on the blanket.

"Dubs," the man across the fire said by way of introduction. "Isn't he something? There are some who have questioned his humanity, thinking he was of another species—men, I should hasten to add, who are not with us any longer, Dubs having sent them to the nether regions—but I do not question him. I am grateful that he is my partner, my right hand. He is Dubs. I am Courtweiler, although most call me simply Court. And you?"

Francis stared at him. Part of his mind was still trying to awaken and part of him was trying to accept that apparently these men meant to harm him. If they had been friendly they would not have taken his rifle. He realized that what had bothered him last night was his acting like an amateur, a greenhorn. He should have placed his bedroll well away from the fire, hidden so he would have time to react if enemies came. Stupid. Well, nothing for it now. He had to buy time, time to think, time to come up with a plan. "Francis," he said. "My name is Francis."

"Ahh—a proper name, that. Francis. I would have liked to have been named Francis but my ancestors came into it and I had to take the family name. Courtweiler isn't bad, but Francis—now that's a name, isn't it, Dubs?"

Francis looked up again and if the giant was listening at all he gave no indication. He held Francis down with one hand while staring out across the prairie.

"It was a stroke of good fortune coming upon you this way," Courtweiler added. "For us, that is. Not so good for you."

"What do you mean?" Francis looked at his rifle, which was across the fire on the ground leaning against Courtweiler's leg while he squatted. He couldn't reach it. And his possibles bag and knife were somewhere in back of him—he'd never get to them before Dubs landed on him.

"I mean, Francis, that we have a specific need for just about everything you have. Our equipment has run into the ground and we aren't halfway to that golden coast we aspire to. I'm afraid we're going to have to relieve you of your belongings."

"My belongings?"

Courtweiler nodded. "Exactly. Gun, horse, saddle—essentially everything. I think I could even fit into that buckskin shirt."

"My clothes, too?"

"Except your pants. I think we'll leave those in the interests of propriety. But everything else. And I don't want you to think I'm ungrateful. Indeed, if you will turn and look," he made a sign to Dubs, who stepped back and let Francis rise, "you will see that I am in desperate straits indeed. Even my mule suffers."

Francis rose to his knees and looked to the rear where an old mule, so skinny its ribs stuck out inches, stood with its head hanging nearly to the ground. On its back was a blanket worn until there were holes through it, no saddle, and instead of a bridle a loop went around the lower jaw. The miracle, Francis thought, was that the mule had gotten this far.

"You see what I mean." Courtweiler pointed to the mule. "Dubs prefers to go afoot, and by the third day will outrun a horse. But given as I am to more intellectual pursuits and less of the physical I need to ride. And so we must have your horse."

"I have kin," Francis said. "Just over that rise. They'll be looking for me . . ."

Courtweiler shook his head. "Dissembling won't help, my boy. We came from there. There are no people there, no tracks, nothing. I do not know how you arrived here but let me assure you, there is nobody close to help you."

"I'll die if you leave me here with nothing."

Courtweiler sighed. "Indeed. There is that possibility. Still, life on the frontier is very hard and we must expect these little setbacks and somehow muddle on, don't you agree? Now, please take off that shirt before I have to ask Dubs to assist you . . ."

Francis hesitated, saw Dubs move and decided not to anger the huge man. He shrugged out of his shirt, felt the morning coolness on his skin.

"Off the blanket, please."

Francis moved from the blanket and Dubs snaked it off the ground and rolled it up in one fluid motion and stood again, still, waiting.

"And now, Francis, as fruitful as it has been to meet you, I'm afraid we must be off . . ."

Dubs had already caught the mare—Francis could not believe they had done all this without awakening him—and they saddled her, left the mule standing and rode off, Courtweiler holding Francis's rifle across his lap as they rode away, headed west while Francis sat next to a dead buffalo, a nearly dead mule, and watched them go.